Jane the Astronaut

The Mystery of the Alien Dragons

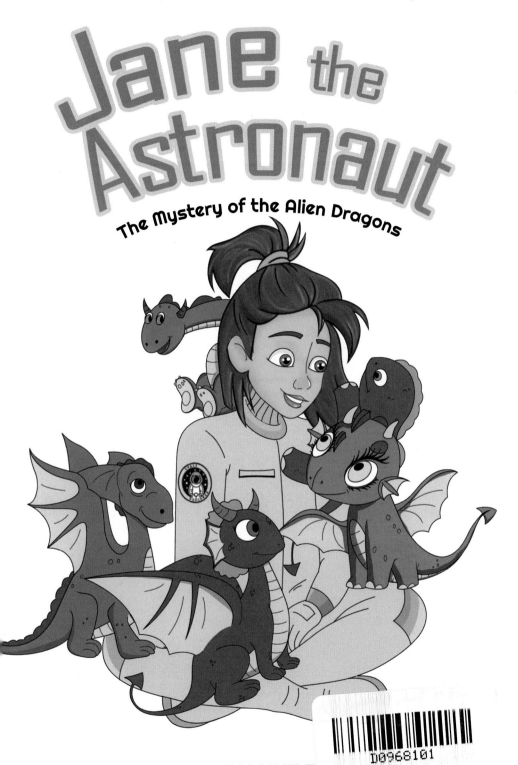

WRITTEN BY DIANNE B

ILLUSTRATED BY REMESH RAM

Jane the Astronaut: The Mystery of the Alien Dragons

Copyright © 2020

Publisher's Cataloging-in-Publication Data

Names: Bateman, Dianne, author. | Remesh, Ram, illustrator.
Title: Jane the astronaut : the mystery of the alien dragons / by Dianne
Bateman ; illustrated by Ram Remesh.
Description: Stuart, FL: The Cat's Secret, 2020. |
Summary: After winning a science contest where first prize is a trip to the
International Space Station, Jane the Astronaut discovers alien dragons
hiding aboard.
Identifiers: LCCN: 2020918692 | ISBN: 978-1-7356658-2-5 (Hardcover) |
978-1-7356658-1-8 (pbk.) | 978-1-7356658-0-1 (ebook)
Subjects: LCSH Dragons--Juvenile fiction. | Space flight--Juvenile fiction. |
Human-alien encounters--Juvenile fiction. | Science fiction.| CYAC
Dragons--Fiction. | Space flight--Fiction. | Human-alien encounters--Fiction.
| BISAC JUVENILE FICTION / Fantasy & Magic | JUVENILE FICTION /
Science Fiction / Alien Contact | JUVENILE FICTION / Science Fiction /
Space Exploration
Classification: LCC PZ7.1.B3765 Jan 2020 | DDC [Fic]--dc23

For copyright permissions, school visits, and book readings/signings, email
dbateman101@yahoo.com.

Written by Dianne Bateman
Illustrated by Remesh Ram
Edited by Bobbie Hinman
Cover design by Praise Saflor
Formatting by Misty Black Media, LLC

ISBN eBook 978-1-7356658-0-1
ISBN Paperback 978-1-7356658-1-8
ISBN Hardback 978-1-7356658-2-5

www.janetheastronaut.com

Contents

For Rowdy and Princess.

Chapter 1

Jane Wins the Contest!

"I won!" announced Jane in a very excited voice.

When she entered the school science contest with her project about "ionizing radiation and the effects of growing plants in outer space," Jane just knew she would win—and she did! Her plan is to someday be both a plant scientist *and* an astronaut—an astrobotanist.

"I'm a teenage astronaut!" Jane said. "Well, not exactly an astronaut…more like an astronaut-in-training. Well, not exactly an astronaut-in-training either."

Her brother Alex gazed at her suspiciously. "You'll never do that," he teased. "You're a girl!."

"Just call me Plant Doc," Jane said, waving a shiny trophy in the air. "I won the contest and I get to spend a whole month on the International Space Station. So there!"

Jane knows everything there is to know about plants. As a matter of fact, she considers herself to be a plant genius. Jane can stick a plant in the soil, smile at it, sing it a song…and it will grow. So when she won the contest and was invited to study the effects of outer space on plants, she screamed in excitement. "YES!" She never even thought it over. She didn't have to.

But before she could go into space, Jane had to prove she was physically fit. Her heart and blood pressure were checked. Perfect! Her vision was checked. Excellent! Her balance was checked. Exceptional! Is she afraid of heights? No! Is she afraid of weightlessness? Of course not! Even the required 4 weeks of training to learn how to live in microgravity didn't scare her. Jane was ready and nothing was going to hold her back.

As excited as she was, how could Jane know what mysterious events lay ahead?

Chapter 2

The Other Passengers

Jane wasn't the only student aboard the Space Station. There were 3 others, all from different countries, and there was the captain and his "real" crew, of course. Sometimes other astronauts came aboard for a few days to check the progress the young scientists were making and offer assistance if needed.

First there was Woody. He had wild, curly hair and after being on the Station for a month, it would probably grow even wilder and curlier. Woody was from England where he was studying Bioastronautics. Everyone called him "Rat Guy" because he tested rats in his lab. Jane knew his work, studying the effects of space on animals, was valuable and might even be used on future missions to Mars.

Hal was the technical guy. He was a computer genius from Australia, a big guy with a loud *HO HO* laugh that made Jane smile every time she heard it. It made her feel like she was working with Santa Clause. Hal seemed to be able to look at computers and know immediately what was wrong with them. He was extremely important to the mission since everything they did depended on computerized equipment. If even one of their computers went kaput, the young scientists would not be able to complete their jobs. Hal worked closely with the captain to keep everything up and running.

Sasha was the only other girl on the space station. She was from Russia and, even though she was quite beautiful, Jane thought Sasha was kind of a nerd. Even so, Jane was happy that there was another girl along. Sasha was so advanced in her studies that she'd probably be a real doctor by the time they landed. Her position was to act as an onboard medical representative. Every day she lined everyone up and did all kinds of doctor stuff, like taking temperatures and blood pressure and listening to everyone's heart. Her experiments and measurements were really gauged to learning about the effects of weightlessness on astronauts' bodies and minds. Her data might even be used for future space missions.

Captain Joe was the commander. He was the only military ranked person onboard, and was in charge of

the entire mission. Captain Joe and his crew were responsible for overseeing the running of the Station, making sure everyone completed their work. He also monitored the security of the mission.

Jane wondered why a security monitor was needed way up in space. "For space aliens and stuff," she thought…and laughed. "Yeah, space aliens—like that would ever happen."

Jane was kept busy on the Space Station, planting different varieties of vegetables and flowers in little containers, subjecting some of them to different wavelengths of light and others to ionizing radiation. She even experimented growing fresh lettuce, thinking how much fun it would be to surprise the crew with a space salad.

Each morning, Jane and her fellow astronauts had breakfast together and shared news about their experiments. They also chatted about how long they had been on the Station and shared stories and jokes about their home countries, which helped keep them from becoming homesick. Woody talked incessantly about his rats; each one had a name. Hal talked about the many kangaroos and crocodiles he had seen back home, while Sasha told stories about how cold it was in Russia and how much she missed her dog. Jane, of course, talked about proving to her brother that girls are just as smart as boys.

Jane had no idea that a wonky machine was about to change the course of her life.

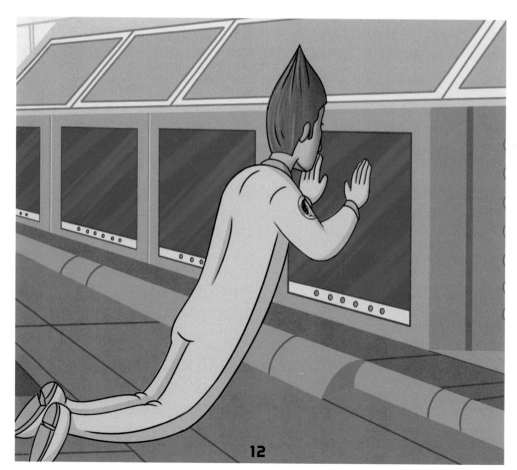

Chapter 3

A Wonky Machine

It was a normal Tuesday—or was it?

Jane left her lab to share some exciting news with her shipmates. She had identified a new photosynthetic organism. Actually, it was exciting to *her*, but the others, as usual, would probably have trouble understanding her scientific babbling. She tidied up, making sure everything was in order before she left her lab.

That's when things started getting wonky. After securing her door, as she started to float down the passage, Jane noticed a large piece of machinery being guided into the lab next door.

"Hey," Jane said. "What's going on?"

Hal's voice came from behind a giant metal box. "Sorry Jane," he said, "I've got to get this computer into the lab and set up for tomorrow. The old one stopped working and Woody won't be able to continue his experiments tomorrow if I don't help. You'll have to go the long way."

"No problem, see you later," said Jane as she waved goodbye, making a detour to avoid bumping into Hal and the big computer.

Jane continued on her way, floating down the passage to find the others. She would look for Sasha first. Jane was moving along as quickly as one can move while weightless…when suddenly she came to an abrupt stop.

There was a DOOR! This was not an airlock; it was an actual DOOR! Jane had worked a lot of hours today so maybe she was tired. Maybe she was imagining this. Maybe she had space fever? She had never heard of space fever, but that didn't mean she didn't have it.

There are no doors on space stations; there are airlocks. But this was definitely a brown wooden door. Jane was flabbergasted. She reached out and touched the door. Yes, it looked like wood…Yes, it felt like wood…Yes, it was a door! How could this be? Jane reached down and touched the old-fashioned-looking, round, brass-colored doorknob, one that looked like it belonged in a haunted house. She touched it. It was cold. She pulled back.

What do you do when an object appears out of nowhere?

Chapter 4

Take a Chance!

Jane always thought of herself as being brave, but should she take this chance? She stared at the door for a long time. A minute went by, then five minutes, then ten minutes…or maybe no time at all…she couldn't tell. Her heart was racing, feeling like it was beating out of her chest. Ever so slowly, she eased closer and closer to the door until her body was right up against it. She reached down, grabbed the knob and turned it. She heard a *click click* and the door opened, very, very slowly…

The light was dim but what she could see was very strange indeed. She was in an office! An old-fashioned office! This was creepy. There were no offices on the space station, but if ever there was one, it certainly wouldn't have an old metal desk and an old wooden chair. The oddest thing about this office was that everything was sitting in the room—in place—as if there was gravity! Nothing was floating around the way it was in the rest of the space station.

How could this be? This room had gravity! How could *this* room have gravity when the rest of the Space Station has microgravity? As she moved a little further into the room, Jane suddenly landed on the floor. *Kerplunk*! Right away her head felt woozy and her stomach was starting to feel icky. She was so used to being weightless and floating all the time that suddenly having her feet on the floor and feeling her full weight was weird.

Jane looked up. Gaudy, old-fashioned lights were hanging from the ceiling, and on the desk was an archaic piece of equipment that she recognized as a *typewriter!* Her dad had told her too many times about the typewriter he used before computers were invented. "Oh my gosh, how can this be?" Jane asked out loud. "I must be imagining all this. It can't possibly be. I'm too tired. I just need to go to bed. That's it."

Jane quickly ran past the brown wooden door and out into the passage where she found herself floating again. Now completely confused and disoriented, she wasn't sure if she was upside down or downside up. Remembering her astronaut training about how to handle unexpected happenings, Jane closed her eyes and calmed herself down. She thought about her home, she thought about her work and she thought about how much she loved being an astronaut. When she opened her eyes, she felt calmer. She reached out and oriented herself by looking at the markings on the wall, then headed in the right direction—back to her room. She bravely dared to glance over her shoulder to take one last look at the door. It was gone!

It *had* been her imagination. She *was* over tired. She *did* need to rest. There *was* no door—or office. But, was she sure?

18

Chapter 5

The next day...

After a good night's sleep, Jane awoke feeling refreshed. She remembered what had happened the night before. Yeah, it was her imagination. She had been tired, that's all. She quickly dressed, then just out of curiosity, decided to take the same passage she had taken last night. She did. There was NO door. As a matter of fact, there were no airlocks at all on that side of the Station, so it was quite odd that she had imagined an office there. She decided to put it out of her mind and get back to her duties and her beloved plants.

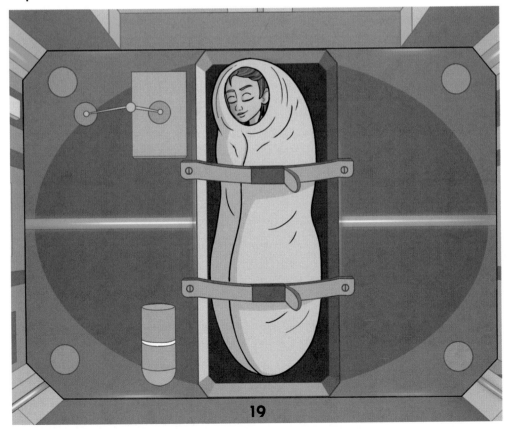

But eerily, that night, once again there was Hal with another piece of equipment.

"Hal," she said, "I see you're back with another computer. Is that for Woody too?"

"Yep," he replied, "for some strange reason, the one I put in last night went kaput today, so here I am with another one. Sorry for the detour, Jane."

Jane smiled and waved goodbye as she once again made a detour and floated along the passage—the same passage she had taken the night before. Not paying too much attention to where she was going, she pulled herself along, thinking only about her favorite ivy plant that wasn't doing well in the radiation Test B. Suddenly she looked up. It was there again…the DOOR!

This time Jane couldn't blame it on being tired, so why was that brown wooden door back? Talking out loud—to no one—Jane said, "If something happens two days in a row, I call that *scientific evidence*. The time has come for a serious investigation."

As Jane opened the door and pulled herself into the strange room once again, *kerplunk!* Gravity! How strange! There she was—standing on the floor. "Maybe this is a figment of my imagination," Jane thought, "but I won't know until I investigate. This *must* be done!"

Taking a deep breath, Jane made her way to the back of the office. She heard a creaking sound and, as she turned to look, she saw what was happening—the door was closing! "No," Jane hollered, hoping someone would hear her. "Oh my gosh, why is it closing?"

She couldn't make her feet move fast enough to get back across the room to the door. It slammed shut with a loud **BANG!**

Chapter 6

Where am I?

Jane looked around. Birds were singing and crickets were chirping. She was standing in a forest with tall trees around her and green grass under her feet. She was both excited and terrified at the same time. "Gosh what do I do now?" she wondered.

But being a brave explorer, Jane gathered her wits and set out to explore. She took a step forward toward the trees, then turned to look back. The office was gone but the door was still there—sitting in the forest all by itself. Where would she go if she needed to make a quick escape?

"Giggle, giggle, giggle," Jane heard. It was coming from the bushes nearby and it sounded like small children, but wasn't that impossible? She was sure of one thing— someone or something was giggling. As Jane edged closer to the bushes, something tiny and pink ran out and grabbed her ankle!

Jane couldn't help screaming, "Hey, what are you doing?"

On the ground beside her was a tiny animal, about the size of a kitten. But it looked more like a dragon than a kitten. It *was* a dragon—and it was giggling! Before she could gather her wits, another similar creature ran out from under the bush. This one was green. It was followed by another and yet another, until she had a rainbow of little dragons in pink, blue, purple and green all hanging onto her and giggling. In fact, they were hanging on so hard that they knocked her off balance and she toppled to the ground.

As Jane screamed, "OUCH," the little dragons jumped back, looking frightened. They made no aggressive moves and seemed as curious about Jane as she was about them. As she sat up, each little dragon came over and gently nuzzled her, much like a kitten or puppy would do. Jane reached out and patted each one on the head. Their skin was soft and shiny—and strangely iridescent—and they seemed to love being touched.

"Where did you come from, little dragons?" Jane asked.

They responded with purring noises.

Jane wondered if the little dragons were young. They seemed plump and well fed, and there was something very childlike about them.

"Oh my gosh!" Jane realized, "I've found extraterrestrial life on the International Space Station!"

The little dragons inched closer to Jane, no longer seeming afraid. She touched their soft skin, realizing that, even though they looked like dragons, it was odd that they didn't feel scaly at all.

But wait a minute, was she *inside* or *outside?* The air felt warm, and plants were growing. There must be water and some type of artificial sunlight to keep the plants and little dragons alive, or had she somehow been transported *off* the Space Station entirely. No, that was not possible. She was *on* the Space Station, just in a room that looked like an office and was filled with little dragons.

Gosh, how loony was this going to sound when she told the others?

Chapter 7

Jane Dreams of Dragons

Jane snuggled and played with the little dragons for hours, not realizing how much time had flown by. "Oh my," she said, looking at her watch, "I have to get some rest. I have work to do." As she stood up to leave, all seven little dragons clung to her, squeaking and squealing. Jane wished she knew how to explain to them that they couldn't go with her. Each time Jane took a few steps, the little dragons ran after her, grabbing her legs.

"No, you can't go. You stay," she said firmly.

After many failed attempts to slip away, Jane was finally able to get the little creatures to stay where they were so she could make her way back to the door. She turned to wave to her friends and was surprised to see them waving back. How could they know how to wave? This added one more crazy thing for Jane to try to figure out. "Bye," she said softly, as she slipped back through the door and into the old office. The grass and trees disappeared. There was just the office—and the brown wooden door—and Jane.

"That was so cool!" whispered Jane.

She floated back to her quarters to rest for a bit before telling her fellow astronauts about what had just happened. Maybe a quick nap would help clear her mind. As soon as Jane put her head down, she fell into a deep sleep. She dreamed about little dragons playing in the grass and climbing on the desk in the magical office that couldn't possibly exist.

It was late when Jane woke up from her nap. "The dragons!" she thought. "I have to tell everyone about the dragons." She tried to guess how they would react. Would they believe her? What if they laughed at her? She had to tell them.

"Hey guys," she said as she floated into the main living area. "You will never guess what I found!" Everyone stopped what they were doing and stared in anticipation as Jane continued. "You see, there's this room on the other side of the Space Station and it has an old-style wooden door…"

Woody, Hal and Sasha looked at her as if they thought it was a joke. Jane excitedly recounted how she found the room and how she went back a second time and found the little animals.

Her friends looked at her in total disbelief. Not a one believed her. Then Hal started to laugh and the others joined in.

"Oh, we didn't know you were such a jokester, Jane," said Hal.

Sad that no one believed her, Jane said, "Fine, then I'll just have show you. Come with me."

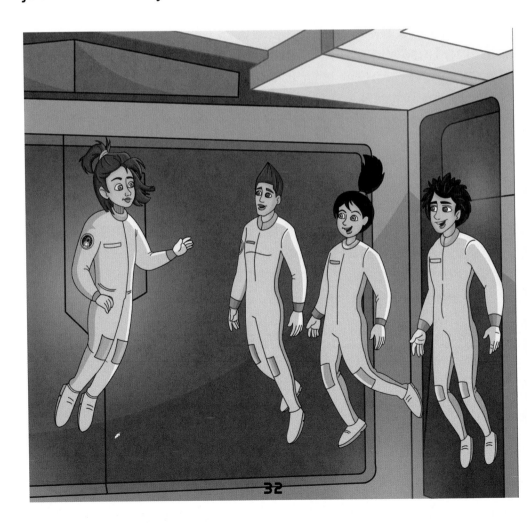

Chapter 8

Jane's Little Joke

Jane led her friends through the passage toward the door. When they arrived, there was...

NO DOOR!

Jane was embarrassed, although she somehow expected this. Had she dreamed every bit of it? Was she really suffering from space sickness? She was sure she had played with the dragons the night before—or had she? What was going on? Was someone playing a cruel trick on her?

Her friends laughed. Sasha said, "That was funny, Jane, "you almost had us believing you."

"Let's all get back to work, now," said Hal.

Feeling totally embarrassed, Jane said, "Yeah guys, I was just pulling your leg—just a little fun and humor. Haha." She left the group and floated straight to her lab.

Jane thought she had handled the situation well. Everyone thought it was a joke, so she would just have to remain secretive and continue her investigation in private. "A covert operation," she thought, smiling.

But unbeknownst to Jane, Captain was worried.

"Hey Woody, got a sec?" he asked.

"Sure, what's up?" Woody was curious.

"Well, do *you* think Jane is okay?" asked Captain.

"Sure Captain, she seems fine. Is there a problem?" Woody moved closer.

The Captain, obviously concerned, said, "I'm just worried about Jane's mental health after that little charade about space dragons."

Woody laughed. "Aw come on, Cap, it was all a joke. Couldn't you tell she was putting us on?"

Now very serious, Captain said, "Woody, do me a favor and keep an eye on her, will you? I'm responsible for you guys and I just want to be sure she's okay. Will you do it?"

"Um, sure thing, Captain," said Woody.

The Captain headed back to Main Controls where he completed his daily reports. In his private logbook he noted:

"Observation of Jane continues after her erratic behavior. At this time there is nothing to report to Command, but making a notation in case this becomes serious."

Realizing that everything that happened on the Space Station was recorded by cameras, the captain pulled the recordings of the day Jane spoke about her space dragons. He watched the feed. There was Jane floating by, then stopping for a few minutes to look out the window before continuing on. Odd, but no space dragons. Well, he thought, he would continue to watch her and if anything else happens, he would have to report her.

It was his responsibility to do this for the safety of the Space Station.

Chapter 9

A return to the dragons

As the days passed, Jane avoided the passage with the mysterious door. But the little dragons started coming to her in her dreams—running to her, grabbing her legs and giggling—always making her feel loved. Their dream visits came more and more frequently, eventually occurring every single night. Each morning she woke up thinking about the little guys and missing them. Jane's family always had cats or a dog, so having pets here reminded her of home.

Jane still continued to avoid that passage. She had felt stupid when her friends laughed at her, and didn't want to remind herself of that day. But it looked like other plans were in store for Jane. Tonight Woody's equipment was broken—yet again—and she would have to go around the big computer once more to get back to her quarters.

As she pushed off, Woody shouted, "Bring me back one of your dragons. I can run some experiments on space dragons instead of space rats." Then he laughed.

Jane floated along, trying her best to ignore Woody's comment. Suddenly, there it was! The brown door! Why did it only appear to *her*? Why couldn't anyone else see it?

Somehow, these little dragons were meant to be Jane's secret and no one else's!

She opened the door and went into the office. As soon as her feet touched the floor, she closed the door and turned to see the beautiful, lush forest.

She called out to her little friends, "Hello little guys, where are you?" Within seconds, Jane could hear the bushes rattling, as out came all 7 dragons, running and giggling. They were hugging her ankles before she knew it. She knelt down, rubbing and hugging each one. They seemed to have grown since the first time Jane saw them. Yes, they were definitely bigger now. She lifted the little pink one, who felt as heavy as a grown cat. She lifted each one and, yes, they were definitely bigger than they had been just a few days ago. She guessed that the lighter ones were females and the heavier ones were males.

Being a scientist, Jane needed to know how these little creatures survived here. Whoever put them here must have provided food and water, but where?

More exploration would be needed.

The little dragons seemed to sense that Jane wanted to look around. They scampered off with Jane in tow. Aha! Behind the bushes was a well-hidden cave. It seemed small at first, but when Jane stepped inside, she realized that it loomed almost 50 feet tall.

"Oh my," Jane exclaimed, her voice echoing in the vast cave. "Does this mean you guys will grow this big?"

The little dragons pulled her over to a nest, hidden in the rocks in the back of the cave. A bed of dried grass made a nice, warm, comfy place to sleep. Jane thought she could hear water splashing. She walked further into the cave and came upon a waterfall,

40

gushing into a pool of clean, clear water. She made a mental note: Next time she would have to remember to bring a test tube with her to get a sample of the water.

Jane now knew where the dragons lived, but what did they eat? Nothing in the cave looked edible and it was definitely too dark for any plants to grow.

Back outside, she wandered around until she came upon a small grove of what appeared to be fruit trees. She recognized several varieties that looked similar to fruits that grew on Earth. One looked a lot like apples, and another like mangos. One unusual bush was loaded with an assortment of red and purple berries. It appeared to Jane that her dragons were vegetarians. If so, they could survive well—as long as nobody disturbed them.

But who left them here and why?

Chapter 10

Trying to Say Goodbye

After hours of exploration, Jane decided it would be best to go back to her quarters. She was falling behind in her work and had really messed up her exercise routine as well, and someone was bound to question what she was up to. Instead of bragging about her little friends, Jane now became worried about the others finding them. She didn't want anyone bothering them. She had to keep them a secret.

Once again, Jane gave each dragon a hug, still amazed at how affectionate they were. When she said goodnight, they seemed to understand that she had to go and that they had to stay. Once again, they waved. Who had taught them how to wave? They were obviously highly intelligent. Jane was fascinated.

"Goodnight little friends," Jane said as she left through the brown wooden door. "Oh my gosh, I've discovered friendly little space aliens!"

Almost every day after work, Jane went to visit the little dragons. They seemed to be growing quickly and were soon up to her knees. Now she had to be careful because when they came to greet her, they often knocked her down. She knew they were friendly and affectionate, but she'd never be able to explain her injuries if she got hurt while playing with them.

Jane still had not found any clues as to where they came from or who left them here.

Her time on the space station was coming to an end. With only 7 days left, she was regretting having to leave the little dragons behind. She tried hard to think of a way she could stay, but there was a time limit for student astronauts, and she knew she had to leave.

What would *they* do without her? Jane wondered if the little dragons would miss her, or if they would just befriend another astronaut when she was gone? She hoped not; she felt they were *her* discovery and they belonged to *her*. But she had no legitimate claim to them—or did she?

That evening, Jane tried her best to explain to the little dragons that her time was coming to an end and that she'd have to leave. They clung to her, seeming to sense her sadness. When Jane started to cry, all 7 dragons made an almost melodic purring sound unlike anything Jane had ever heard. They circled around her as if trying to ease her sadness.

When Jane left that night, the little dragons didn't wave.

Chapter 11

Shuttle to Earth

The next day, Jane received new orders containing several experiments that had to be completed before she could leave the Space Station. She was too busy to visit the little dragons and she was fearful that she wouldn't be able to see them for one more final goodbye. She knew her priority had to be her job as an astronaut, and that had to come first.

It seemed impossible to Jane that she was facing her last night at the space station. The month had flown by. She knew the shuttle was scheduled to dock in a few

hours, transporting the young astronauts back to Earth. She and Woody were scheduled to leave first. The others would follow on the next shuttle. Was there time to see her little dragons...just for a few minutes?

When Jane was sure no one was looking, she floated along the passage toward the door, but there was...

NO DOOR!

Jane was in a panic. What had happened? Were the dragons gone? Could they just be hiding? Maybe they had already found a new friend and no longer cared for her. She was befuddled. She felt crushed. Where were the little dragons?

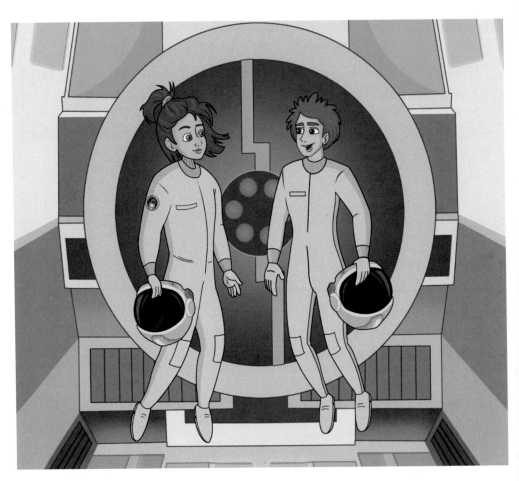

After a sleepless night, Jane put on her space suit, took her personal belongings and boarded the shuttle for home. She tried to concentrate on the excitement of flying on the space shuttle again, but her heart was still broken. What had happened to her little dragons?

After landing, Jane and Woody were quarantined at the Air Force Base, a normal procedure for returning astronauts. That night, Jane dreamed of the little dragons. They were hugging her. Maybe someday she would find a way to see them again.

Did the dragons live only in Jane's dreams? Would Jane ever see them again?

About the Author:

Dianne Bateman wrote her first book at 16 but was too shy to share with others. With the birth of her child and grandchild she devoted much time to reading and passed along that love for children's adventure stories.

After retiring from a successful business career, Dianne began to share her adventures of Rowdy and Princess - her beloved cats which created a large following.

Her fans encouraged her to write a children's book and the idea for Jane the Astronaut was born!

Visit janetheastronaut.com to sign up for Dianne's VIP list and receive free downloads and other bonus materials.

Follow Dianne on social media.

Facebook.com/
diannebatemanauthor

Instagram.com/
diannebatemanbooks

Janetheastronaut.com

Look for the companion coloring book!

Made in the USA
Middletown, DE
03 December 2021

54020450R00029